Marmalade's Picnic

by Cindy Wheeler

Alfred A. Knopf, New York

FOR DINAH

This is a Borzoi Book published by Alfred A. Knopf, Inc.

Copyright © 1983 by Cindy Wheeler

All rights reserved under International and Pan-American Copyright Conventions.
Published in the United States by Alfred A. Knopf, Inc., New York,
and simultaneously in Canada by Random House of Canada Limited, Toronto.
Distributed by Random House, Inc., New York.
Manufactured in the United States of America
2 4 6 8 10 9 7 5 3

Library of Congress Cataloging in Publication Data
Wheeler, Cindy. Marmalade's picnic.
Summary: Marmalade the cat finds a satisfying way to accompany
his owner on a picnic.
[1. Cats—Fiction] I. Title.
PZ7.W5593Mar 1982 [E] 81-20792
ISBN 0-394-85023-8 AACR2 ISBN 0-394-95023-2 (lib. bdg.)

It's a beautiful morning.

Marmalade is awake.

Time to get up!

O.K., Marmalade!

This is a nice day for a picnic.

The picnic is ready.

Now, food for Marmalade.

Where is Marmalade?

Marmalade does not want cat food.

He wants the picnic food.

Marmalade is going on the picnic, too.

Here is a good place to stop.

Time for lunch.

What a good picnic!

Cindy Wheeler grew up in Alabama, Virginia, and North Carolina. After receiving a B.F.A. degree from Auburn University, Ms. Wheeler worked for a bookseller and for a publisher. Now she devotes full time to writing and illustrating children's books.

Ms. Wheeler lives in Cold Spring, New York, with her husband and one black cat.